Pooch Parlour

Wedding Tails

For Lauren, Alex and Charlotte - KC

For Chrissie and Ali - JAD

STRIPES PUBLISHING
An imprint of Little Tiger Press
1 The Coda Centre, 189 Munster Road,
London SW6 6AW

This paperback edition first published
in Great Britain in 2015.

Text copyright © Katy Cannon, 2015
Illustrations copyright © Artful Doodlers, 2015
Cover illustration copyright © Simon Mendez, 2015

ISBN: 978-1-84715-510-8

A CIP catalogue record for this book is available
from the British Library.

Printed and bound in the UK.

2 4 6 8 10 9 7 5 3 1

Wedding Tails

Katy Cannon

Stripes

Chapter One

Abi bounced excitedly in the passenger seat of the pink Pooch Parlour van. She'd been looking forward to this day all summer – the day of the most exciting (and dog-friendly) wedding of the year! Pop star Maria was getting married to celebrity chef Joey Henshaw that afternoon. They had met while they were both walking their pet Dalmatians in the local park, and now those same dogs would be the ring bearers at their wedding!

Most wonderful of all, Maria and Joey had asked Abi's Aunt Tiffany to bring the staff of her luxury dog-grooming salon, Pooch Parlour, to the hotel to groom all the dogs attending the wedding. And since Abi was helping at Pooch Parlour for the summer, she got to go too!

On the back seat of the van, Hugo the miniature dachshund and Abi's dog Lulu, a bichon frise, were in their travel crate ready for the drive. Aunt Tiffany had explained that travelling in the crate would keep them calm and safe during the journey and stop them from distracting her while she drove. They had plenty of space, though, and at that moment they were both snuggled down, looking ready for the journey. The dogs were dressed in special pink T-shirts with the Pooch Parlour logo on them – Mel, the wardrobe mistress, had ordered them especially for the big day!

The back of the van was filled with boxes of things they needed to set up a mobile Pooch Parlour at the wedding venue. Abi bit her lip as she thought about what a busy — but brilliant — day they had ahead of them.

"Right! We're ready to go," Aunt Tiffany said, climbing into the driver's seat. "Mel, Rebecca and Kim will be wondering what's happened to us! They left almost half an hour ago."

"Will it take long to get there?" Abi asked, as Aunt Tiffany started the engine.

"About an hour," Aunt Tiffany said.

Abi stared out of the window as they drove, watching the busy streets and tall buildings of central London slowly fade into green fields and countryside. The dogs were so quiet that Abi suspected they had fallen asleep. She thought about closing her eyes — but she was far too excited to snooze!

Finally, after what seemed like hours, Abi spotted the Washington House Hotel. It was the grandest, most beautiful house she'd ever seen, with ivy climbing up its walls and a wood spreading out behind the building.

Aunt Tiffany's pink van came to a stop at the top of the long drive, in front of the hotel. Abi stepped out and looked up at the ivy and the countless windows and the chimneys that ran all along the roof. The Washington House Hotel looked even grander from close up!

Aunt Tiffany went to talk to a man in uniform, so Abi opened the travel crate and let Lulu and Hugo jump down. She clipped leads on to both the dogs, just in case. Abi didn't think either of them would run off, but she didn't want to take any chances today.

With the dogs panting at her feet in the hot sun, Abi stood back and took in the amazing view around the hotel. Surrounded by fields and trees, she could hardly believe that they were so close to London.

"This place is incredible," Abi whispered.

"Isn't it?"

Abi looked up to see a younger girl wearing shorts and a T-shirt standing on the steps to the front door of the hotel. She had blonde hair in bunches, and freckles all over her nose.

"I think this is the best place I've ever been. Ever! I'm Molly, by the way. I'm one of the bridesmaids – Maria's my sister."

Molly was a bit shorter than she was, and Abi guessed her to be about seven. She smiled as Molly came down the steps, skipping with excitement.

"I'm Abi," Abi said, laughing as Lulu barked at her feet. "And this is Lulu. We're here with my aunt Tiffany – and this little guy is Hugo. Aunt Tiffany runs Pooch Parlour. She's responsible for grooming and dressing all the dogs today, and running the Doggy Daycare. And I get to help out." She couldn't help but smile with a bit of pride when she said that.

"*Really?*" Molly breathed. "Oh my gosh, I love dogs! That must be the most exciting job in the world!"

"It is," Abi said happily. "When I grow up,

I want to work with animals too. Aunt Tiffany says that helping out at Pooch Parlour this summer will be good practice!"

"Wow!" Molly looked very impressed. Abi thought it was funny that a girl who was bridesmaid at the biggest wedding of the year was excited by the idea of looking after dogs. "I really, really wish I could help too. Do you think your aunt would let me?"

"I don't know," Abi said. Molly seemed very keen and eager to help, and she said she loved dogs. "But I can ask her!"

Chapter Two

Molly bounced up and down on the spot, her hands clasped together in front of her. "Would you? That would be so great! I mean, I know the wedding will be exciting, but right now everyone's just getting ready and there's nothing for me to do and it's, well…" She looked around, as if to make sure no one else was listening, then leaned in towards Abi. "It's kind of boring," she whispered.

Abi grinned. "Come on," she said. "That's Aunt Tiffany over there, talking to the hotel staff. Let's go and ask her."

Molly's eyes grew wide. "*That's* your aunt? She's very glamorous."

"She is. But she's very nice," Abi assured the younger girl. "Come on."

Tugging Molly's hand she led her over to Aunt Tiffany, with Hugo and Lulu's leads in her other hand.

Over by the van, Aunt Tiffany had just finished talking to a man in uniform and a lady in a suit when Abi and Molly arrived.

"Right Abi, let's go and get set up," Aunt Tiffany said, then smiled as she spotted Molly. "Hello. Who's this?"

"This is Molly, Maria's sister," Abi explained. "She's going to be a bridesmaid later, but there's nothing for her to do right now.

Do you think that maybe she could help us for a while?"

"Well, that depends." Aunt Tiffany turned to Molly, bending slightly as she spoke to the younger girl. "Firstly, do you like dogs?" Molly nodded, looking very serious. "And do dogs like you?" Molly nodded again, even harder.

Aunt Tiffany straightened up and smiled. "In that case, I think you'd be a perfect addition to the Pooch Parlour team for the day!"

Molly did a little jump in excitement. "Thank you, thank you, thank you! I'll be the best helper you ever had! Well, apart from Abi, of course. I'm sure Abi's better than me because she's had more practice. But I'll be the second-best helper ever, ever!" Molly's words all ran into each other she spoke so fast and Abi couldn't help but laugh.

"Here, why don't you take Hugo's lead?" Abi suggested, offering it to Molly.

"OK!" Molly grabbed it from Abi's hand and started skipping ahead, Hugo scampering alongside to keep up. But after a few steps, Molly stopped and turned back to face them. "Um, where are we going?"

"We've been assigned a room at the back of the hotel for the Daycare," Aunt Tiffany said, with a laugh. "The other Pooch Parlour van is already round there unloading, and the hotel staff are going to take our things over. Come on, I'll show you."

Aunt Tiffany led them round the side of the hotel, past some pretty flowering bushes and along the edge of the wood, until they reached a fenced-in area with a gate to it. Lulu barked when she saw Rebecca setting out dog toys on the grass.

"You're here!" Rebecca cried, glancing up and smiling at them. "We're just getting everything ready. And it seems like we have a new helper," she added, looking at Molly.

"This is Molly," Abi explained. "She's Maria's sister, and she's going to help out until it's time for her to put on her bridesmaid's dress."

"Great!" Rebecca said. "Why don't you let Lulu and Hugo play out here, and I'll show you both round while Tiffany checks the Doggy Spa set-up. Then she can tell you what she needs help with today."

Abi nodded and bent down to let Lulu off her lead now they were safely inside the Pooch Parlour area. Molly did the same for Hugo, then whispered to Abi, "What's a Doggy Spa?"

"It's where the dogs get washed and combed and trimmed," Abi explained. "Back at Pooch Parlour we have a whole room for it, with a special bone-shaped bath and everything."

"How are they going to do all that here?" Molly asked.

"I guess we're going to find out!" Abi said, watching Lulu and Hugo scamper off to play with a Treat Tumbler.

Chapter Three

"This fenced-in area is where the dogs can play and work off some energy before the wedding," Rebecca explained to Abi and Molly. "We've brought plenty of things to keep them entertained. But all the important stuff will be happening in here." Rebecca opened a set of double doors that led into a large room, split into three different areas.

"This part looks just like the Doggy Daycare back at Pooch Parlour," Abi said, amazed. There were cosy dog beds, indoor toys and a feeding station set up along one wall.

"That's the idea!" Rebecca said. "It's a good job the Washington House Hotel prides itself on being dog-friendly. There are going to be a lot of dogs here today!"

"So you're going to be looking after all the dogs while the wedding is going on?" Molly asked.

Rebecca nodded. "Maria wants the dogs to be part of the wedding service itself, but afterwards, once you all go for dinner, the dogs are going to come back here and have their own feast and a chance to play."

"But first we have to get all of them ready for the wedding itself," Aunt Tiffany said, emerging from behind a screen at one side of the room.

"Come and see."

Abi and Molly followed Aunt Tiffany behind the screen.

"This is the Doggy Spa for the day," Aunt Tiffany said, spreading her arms to show off the area they'd set up for grooming the dogs. "It's not quite as fancy as at Pooch Parlour…"

"No bone-shaped bath," Molly said with a serious face, as if she knew everything about it. Abi hid a smile.

"But it should do for today," Aunt Tiffany finished. "Most of the dogs have been to the parlour recently to be bathed and fully groomed – we wouldn't have time to do them all this morning, anyway. But we've got the portable grooming tables set up for last-minute trims and tidy-ups, and I have a puppy bath or two we can fill up in the bathroom next door for any emergencies!"

"So, this is where the dogs will come first?" Abi asked.

Aunt Tiffany nodded. "We've suggested that the guests bring their dogs here as soon as they arrive. That way, we can prepare them while the guests go and get ready for the wedding. Then they'll be picked up in time for the ceremony."

Molly had begun investigating one of the grooming stations, flicking the bristles of a brush they used for longer-haired dogs, and reading the names on some of the  bottles of scented finishing spray that kept the dogs' coats shiny and smelling sweet.

"These are brilliant!" Molly said. "Does coconut coat spray really smell like coconuts?"

She started to pull the top off the spray bottle to find out, but Aunt Tiffany took it from her.

"Maybe we can find out later, once the dogs are here," she said, smiling gently. "But first, there's more to see. Come on!"

Aunt Tiffany took them over to the other side of the room, where an area had been blocked off using a table with a long cloth over it.

"Oh, and this is where we're going to dress the dogs!" Abi said, spotting the rack of doggy outfits hanging behind Mel, Pooch Parlour's wardrobe mistress. There was also a bucket of treats, ready for rewarding the dogs for behaving while they had their outfits put on. Abi realized that Mel had chosen the least messy treats possible – no one wanted the dogs to get mucky after all the time and effort they'd put in to make them look great!

"That's right," Mel said. "Take a look."

"Some of the dogs have full outfits," Mel explained, "and others are just wearing fancy collars or bows, but they're all going to look fabulous! Are you going to be helping me again?"

"I think so," Abi answered. She liked helping Mel and had got plenty of practice at dressing dogs at a recent charity fashion show. "Aunt Tiffany, do you have anything else you need me to do?"

"Can I help too?" Molly asked, bouncing on her toes. "These outfits look even more fun than the sprays and things." She darted past Mel to the rail of outfits and began looking through them all.

Aunt Tiffany laughed. "Yes, you can both help Mel. But not right now – it won't be time for the dogs to put on those outfits for a little while yet."

Molly stopped investigating the clothes rail and turned back to face them. "Why not?"

"Because we don't want them to get their wedding outfits dirty by playing in them before the ceremony, right?" Abi guessed.

"Just like me and my bridesmaid's dress," Molly added. "Mum says I can't put that on until the very last minute." She rolled her eyes. "She thinks I'll get jam on it, or something. I don't even know where there *is* any jam in this place!"

Aunt Tiffany smiled. "I don't know about jam, Molly, but yes, that's why. We want the dogs to be able to play outside and have fun while they're here, so we don't want to be worrying about their outfits."

"But if they're going to be groomed as soon as they arrive, how will we stop them getting their coats mucky *before* they put their outfits on?" Abi asked, frowning.

"Actually, that's going to be yours and Molly's job this morning."

Chapter Four

Abi and Molly looked at each other in horror. Keep all those dogs clean and tidy at once? It sounded like an impossible task.

Abi's alarm must have shown on her face, because Aunt Tiffany laughed and said, "Don't worry. We've bought some special overcoats for them to wear, to keep them neat and clean. All you and Molly need to do is put them on so they can play until it's time to change into their wedding outfits."

Abi let out a sigh of relief. Dressing dogs she could do. Keeping twenty or more dogs out of mucky puddles, bowls of food and dirt patches would be a lot harder! "I think I can manage that," she told her aunt, and Tiffany smiled.

"I knew I could rely on you, Abi," she said. "The jackets are over here."

Abi and Molly followed Aunt Tiffany to where several boxes had been stored in one corner of the dressing area. They were filled with what looked like waterproof raincoats.

Aunt Tiffany pointed to the box on the end. "They're all sorted by size," she explained. "From small at that end to large at this. Why don't you two practise putting one on Hugo or Lulu?"

At the mention of his name, Hugo pottered in through the doors.

"Hugo!" Molly cried, like they were old friends. She tried to hug him but Hugo, a little alarmed by her enthusiasm, shuffled back again.

"Here, Hugo, come here, boy," Abi called, and the dachshund padded over to her.

Molly looked a little disappointed, so Abi said, "Molly, do you want to see if you can find an overcoat the right size for Hugo?"

Molly started rooting through the boxes straight away, finally holding up a Hugo-sized overcoat in triumph. "Can I put it on him?"

"Do you know how?" Abi asked.

Molly shrugged. "How hard can it be?"

"Trickier than you'd think!" Abi remembered her best friend, Emily, trying to dress dogs for the first time at a fashion show earlier in the summer. It had taken a lot of practice before she'd been able to do it easily! "Tell you what, I'll show you how to do it with Hugo, then you can try. OK?"

Abi got down on to the floor next to Hugo and Molly sat down cross-legged to watch as Abi opened up the Velcro that would fasten underneath Hugo's belly. Carefully, Abi slipped Hugo's little legs through the arm holes, fastened the Velcro, and made sure the loop around his tail was secure at the back.

"There you go! Nothing to it," Abi said, and Molly grinned.

"My turn!" she said.

But just then, the door opened and a man entered, holding the leads of two beautiful Dalmatians.

"Joey!" Molly cried, and raced over to hug him. Then she crouched down to hug the dogs too. "Hello, Polka! Hello, Smudge!"

"Good morning, Mr Henshaw," Aunt Tiffany said, as she and Abi walked across to him.

"Call me Joey," he said, with a smile. "And you must be Tiffany? Maria tells me that you are the only person to trust with looking after all our precious pets today."

"We'll take the very best care of them," Aunt Tiffany replied.

"And guess what, Joey?" Molly bounced back up again. "I'm going to help! Abi and I are going to keep the dogs clean and play with them until it's time for them to put their outfits on!"

"Wow! That sounds like fun," Joey said. "And I know Polka will like having you here." He looked at Aunt Tiffany. "She's been a bit restless this morning, I'm afraid. She's not used to being apart from Maria. Neither am I, actually," he added. "But Maria says it's bad luck for the groom to see the bride before the wedding, so I'm staying out of her way!"

"Probably for the best," Aunt Tiffany agreed. "I'm sure you want everything to go smoothly today."

"Definitely!" Joey said. "Here are the rings, ready for Polka and Smudge later." He handed Aunt Tiffany two small velvet boxes. "Take good care of them!"

"Of course we will. Do you mind if I check the rings?" Aunt Tiffany opened the boxes, and Abi gasped in delight. "They're beautiful," Aunt Tiffany said. "I'll put them in a very safe place until it's time for the ceremony."

Abi couldn't wait to see the two Dalmatians with the rings tied on ribbons around their necks. They were going to walk down the aisle before Maria, then wait at the side ready for the moment when Maria and Joey would exchange wedding rings.

"Perfect," Joey said. "Now, if you ladies have all you need, I'd better go and make sure everything else is ready."

"And here come our next guests, I think," Aunt Tiffany said.

The door opened again, and Abi stared as a woman brought in a gigantic Irish wolfhound. Behind her was a man with two tiny chihuahuas, then another man with a lovely chocolate Labrador. The queue went all the way down the corridor.

It was going to be a very busy morning!

Chapter Five

While Aunt Tiffany and Kim started grooming the dogs, Rebecca kept the dogs entertained as they waited, and Mel helped Molly and Abi with the overcoats.

Polka and Smudge were ready for their jackets first. Dalmatians, with their short coats, didn't usually take a lot of grooming, but they did need regular brushing, and today Polka and Smudge had been brushed until they gleamed.

"Can I do Polka's coat?" Molly asked, jumping up as Kim brought the Dalmatians over. Polka and Smudge danced across the floor of the Doggy Daycare, caught up in the infectious excitement of the day as much as the humans were. "I didn't get to try putting one on Hugo in the end."

"OK," Abi said. After all, it might be easier for Molly to start with a dog who knew her well. "I'll help."

"And I'll take care of Smudge," Mel said, with a smile as she pulled out two of the larger overcoats and passed one to Molly.

Kim rushed back to help Aunt Tiffany with the next dogs.

"Isn't it all so romantic?" Mel sighed, as they started to dress Polka and Smudge. Polka's coat was bright and clean in the white patches, and glossy black for her spots. "The wedding, I mean.

But also how they met! Maria was just walking Polka in the park one day, when this naughty girl ran off after another Dalmatian!" She rubbed a hand affectionately over Smudge's head as she spoke. "Of course, it all worked out for the best in the end. Because if Polka hadn't chased after Smudge, Maria would never have met Joey."

Abi smiled. She loved the idea of dogs bringing people together. Mel was right. It *was* very romantic.

"I like Joey," Molly said, as she carefully lifted Polka's front leg to ease it through the armhole of the jacket. Abi reached over to help guide the dog's leg through. "And Polka likes him too. Polka's good at knowing whether people are nice or not, just by sniffing them, you know. Dalmatians have an excellent sense of smell, Maria says."

"Is she a trained tracker?" Mel asked.

Molly shrugged. "I don't know. But she's good at finding things. Polka usually finds stuff behind the sofa."

"There you are, boy. You go and play, now," Mel said, as she finished putting on Smudge's overcoat. "I can't wait to see Maria's wedding dress," she added.

"It's white," Molly said, and Mel laughed.

Abi couldn't wait to see Maria's dress either – it had been kept very hush-hush, according to Abi's friend Emily. Emily always knew these things because her mum read the celebrity magazines.

Molly finished dressing Polka, and the Dalmatian followed Smudge, who had found Lulu playing with a squeaky-bone toy. Both Dalmatians were far bigger than the little bichon frise, even though they were only young dogs.

It was easy to tell the two Dalmatians apart, Abi noticed, as she watched them walking side by side. Smudge's spots were less crisp and defined around the edges than Polka's, almost like he'd been rolling in dust.

Kim brought over the next two dogs, and Mel, Abi and Molly dressed them in their overcoats too.

After nearly twenty dogs, Molly was getting distracted.

"Molly, do you want to go and play with some of the dogs outside?" Abi asked, when Molly knocked over one of the boxes of overcoats.

"Yes, please!" Molly jumped to her feet. Then she stopped. "Unless you need me to help you…"

Abi smiled. Molly really did want to help, but she *was* only seven and Abi knew that playing with the dogs was more fun than dressing them. "I think I can manage."

"OK!" Molly dashed outside, and Abi heard some barks of welcome from the dogs playing in the fenced-in area with Rebecca.

Mel and Abi carried on dressing the dogs,

with Aunt Tiffany and Kim helping too once they'd finished the grooming.

Finally the last dog — a greyhound called Flash — was safely covered by his overcoat. Now all they had to do was wait until it was time to start putting the dogs in their wedding outfits.

"What do you want me to do now, Aunt Tiffany?" Abi asked. Secretly, she was hoping she'd get to go and play outside with the dogs too!

"Well, I think we can— Goodness!" Aunt Tiffany put her hand to her mouth and her eyes widened. Abi turned quickly to see what had alarmed her.

There in the doorway, trailing muddy pawprints across the carpet, was Smudge. He wasn't wearing his protective overcoat and he was so filthy, it was hard to tell which parts of the Dalmatian's coat were spots and which were dirt!

Chapter Six

"Oh no! What happened?" Abi asked, as Molly came running in after the Dalmatian, holding his overcoat in her hands.

"I'm sorry!" Molly looked truly miserable. "He looked hot and he was scratching at his belly, so I took his overcoat off – but then he dashed straight for that muddy patch in the corner and started digging. Am I in trouble?"

Part of Abi thought that maybe Molly *should* be in trouble, but she quickly told herself the thought was unkind. Molly had only been trying to take good care of Smudge, and dogs *did* like to dig. It couldn't be helped now, anyway.

"You're not in trouble, Molly," Aunt Tiffany said, her voice calm and soothing. "In fact, you can continue to help by looking after the other dogs with Rebecca and Abi, while I brush out Smudge's coat to make sure he's clean and tidy again for the wedding."

Molly nodded. "I will. I'll take really good care of them, I promise!"

"Just don't take their overcoats off," Aunt Tiffany joked, as her phone started to ring. She pulled it from her pocket and answered it. "Hello? Pooch Parlour. Hello, Maria. Yes, everything is just fine down here, don't worry. Polka's having a lovely time." She listened for a moment, then smiled. "Of course you can. I'll send someone to show you where we are now."

As she hung up, she turned to Abi. "I have a new and very important job for you," she said. "I need you to go up to the bridal suite and bring Maria down to check on Polka. Do you think you can manage?"

Manage talking to a real pop star? Abi grinned with excitement. "Of course I can!"

Aunt Tiffany gave Abi instructions on how to find the bridal suite, where Maria was getting ready, and Abi and Lulu trotted off together. They walked through the hotel, past people carrying huge flower arrangements, a man with a double bass, and a room filled with tables and chairs with ribbons tied to them. Once they reached the lobby, they climbed the very grand staircase at the centre of the hotel, then turned left along the first-floor corridor, as Aunt Tiffany had described.

"I hope there's a sign or something," Abi muttered to Lulu. She felt very out of place in her casual clothes. How would she know which room Maria was in if there wasn't a sign?

But as they reached the end of the corridor, Abi heard laughing and chattering voices. This had to be the right place, she thought, even before she spotted the small plaque beside the door that read "Bridal Suite".

She knocked timidly, but nobody answered. Maybe they hadn't heard her ... or maybe they didn't want to be disturbed! Except Aunt Tiffany *had* said that she'd send someone up. Gathering her courage and hoping she wasn't about to annoy a world-famous pop star on her wedding day, Abi knocked again, louder.

This time, the door sprung open quickly to reveal Maria, fully made up and with her hair arranged in dark curls, finished off by a short lace veil. It looked a little strange worn with jeans and a blouse.

"Oh, hello!" Maria said, beaming. "Are you here to take me to see Polka?"

"I am," Abi said, and Lulu barked in agreement.

"Fantastic! Back soon, ladies." Maria waved into the room and Abi spotted several other women standing next to a rail of rose-pink bridesmaid dresses. "My bridesmaids," Maria explained, as Abi started to lead her back the way she'd come. "Well, all but one of them, anyway. My little sister—"

"Molly," Abi finished for her. "She's downstairs helping us in the Doggy Daycare."

"That's brilliant!" Maria said, clapping her hands together. "I was so worried she'd be bored. Molly does like to help out, but there's really not much for her to do for the wedding today. And when she gets bored, she tends to start investigating, or fiddling with things…"

Abi thought about Smudge and his muddy coat. "I'm sure she'll be fine with Aunt Tiffany," she said. After all, Molly seemed to have learned her lesson about how to look after the dogs.

"Thank you for coming to get me," Maria said. "Polka and I are very close, so she gets a little unsettled if she hasn't seen me for a while, and she spent last night with Joey and Smudge, you see. I thought that if I came and helped her get used to the Doggie Daycare, she wouldn't come looking for me!"

"That's a good idea," Abi replied. Joey had said the same thing about Polka. "It's just this way," she added, as they reached the bottom of the grand staircase.

Maria stopped suddenly, statue-still, her eyes wide. "Oh no. We can't go that way."

Abi blinked. "Um ... why not?" Was this some sort of rule she didn't know about?

"That's where everyone's getting ready for the wedding!" Maria said. Without waiting for Abi, she ducked round the corner and out through a side door. With Lulu at her heels, Abi followed quickly.

Outside, Maria stood beside the wall of the hotel. "I'm sorry," she said, with an apologetic smile. "But it's very important that I don't bump into Joey. It's terribly bad luck for the groom to see the bride on the morning of the wedding. Especially since I'm already wearing my veil."

Of course! Joey had mentioned that too. "That's OK. We can probably walk round the back of the hotel from here to the Daycare, past the gardens and round the edge of the woods. We walked that way earlier, and I don't think anyone from the wedding will be there right now, do you?"

Maria grinned. "You're right! It'll be like a secret mission." Putting a hand to her head she adjusted her veil. "Does that look straight? It keeps slipping. It's silly to wear it, I suppose, but it belonged to my grandma, and she's desperate to see me wear it today."

"It looks lovely," Abi said truthfully.

"Come on, then," Maria said. "Let's go."

Maria and Abi kept to the edge of the gardens as they walked round to the woods and the back of the hotel. The scent from the flower bushes was sweet and the breeze was cool, and

Lulu found plenty of small insects to chase.

"Once I know that Polka is settled, I'll be able to properly relax and enjoy my day," Maria said.

"She's been fine this morning," Abi reassured the pop star. "Especially with Molly and Smudge there to keep her company."

"Molly's great with her. And Polka does love Smudge," Maria said fondly. "Almost as much as I love his owner." Then her eyes widened and she grabbed Abi's arm, dragging her into the garden closest to the Daycare.

"What—?" Abi started, but Maria hushed her.

"Joey," she breathed into Abi's ear, pointing towards the hotel.

Chapter Seven

Abi looked where Maria had pointed and saw Joey strolling towards them along the path.

"He can't see me!" Maria whispered urgently. "Not until the wedding!"

But Joey seemed to be heading directly their way and, suddenly, Lulu darted out after a butterfly. Oh no! Joey would be sure to see them now. There was only one thing for it.

"I'll go and distract him," Abi said. "Then you can sneak back through the gardens and into the hotel by the side door. I'm sorry you didn't get to see Polka."

Maria nodded. "I'll try and make it down again later, if I can."

Abi followed Lulu, shortening her lead to keep her closer at heel. Joey looked up as they emerged from behind the bush where Maria was hiding and smiled.

"Hello again!" he said cheerfully. Abi could see how he and Maria had become friends the moment their dogs met. It was hard not to smile back at Joey. "Just the pair I was looking for! I need a little bit of help with something – do you think your aunt can spare you to give me a hand?" He bent down to pet Lulu, who pushed her nose against his hand approvingly.

Abi smiled. "Let's ask!" she said, leading him

away from Maria's hiding place and towards the gate where the Doggie Daycare had been set up.

She glanced back once as they went, and spotted Maria's dark curls darting out from between the bushes, heading through the gardens towards the hotel's side entrance.

Phew. That was a close call! Abi thought.

Aunt Tiffany said it was fine, although she looked a little confused to see Abi return with the groom, instead of the bride! Abi whispered that she'd explain later, then followed Joey round to a beautiful garden on the other side of the hotel. There was a large grassy area set out with rows of pretty white chairs, and a wide aisle running down the centre. The chairs were decorated with posies of wildflowers, and at the front of the aisle was a wooden arch with more

flowers woven in and out of the gaps, all the
way over. It was beautiful!

"Wow!" Abi said. "Is this where the wedding
will be?"

Joey nodded. "And you see those cushions?"

Abi spotted the line of pink cushions set out between each row of chairs. "They're for the guests' dogs to sit on, during the ceremony. We wanted the pooches to be as much a part of our big day as their owners."

"I think that's a lovely idea," Abi said.

"And to stop the dogs getting bored, we ordered a treat bag to go on each cushion." Joey moved to the back row of chairs and lifted a large cardboard box, carrying it over to where Abi and Lulu were waiting. "They were supposed to arrive first thing this morning, but the van delivering them broke down so they've only just got here. Can you help me set them out on the cushions? Any leftovers we can take back to the Doggy Daycare, if you like."

"That sounds great – of course I'll help." Abi picked the first treat bag out of the box and peered inside. "Ooh, the dogs will love these!"

Inside the treat bags were squeaky toys, Barker's Bites snacks and rawhide chews that looked like horseshoes. They'd be perfect for the doggy guests!

Joey grinned. "I'm glad you approve! Now we just need to put one of these on every cushion." He paused. "And there are a lot of cushions."

"Then we'd better get started!" Abi grabbed a handful of bags, and set off for the nearest row.

With both of them working together, it didn't take *too* long – although there were a lot of cushions!

"Remind me why we invited so many people?" Joey joked at one point.

"Because it's the biggest celebrity wedding of the year?" Abi guessed, and Joey laughed.

"I suppose that's it!"

Eventually, every cushion had a treat bag, and there were still a few left in the box. Joey took one out and, very seriously, bowed to Lulu and placed it on the floor in front of her. She barked and hopped forward to investigate.

Giggling, Abi knelt down and helped Lulu open the bag. Lulu pushed her nose against the edge of the bag until a couple of Barker's Bites fell out, then she gobbled them down. Abi picked up the bag and closed it again.

"Maybe we'll save the rest for later, huh, Lulu?"

Joey lifted the box again. "Come on. Let's get these back to the Daycare, then I'd better go and start getting ready myself!"

"Thanks again for your help," Joey said, as they turned the corner of the hotel. Abi could see the Daycare up ahead. There was no sign of Maria, though.

"No problem," Abi said, stepping forward towards the fence. Joey followed with the box and Lulu scampered at Abi's feet. "I think the treat bags are a great idea. The wedding is going to brilliant!"

But then she realized that the gate to the Daycare was open…

Chapter Eight

"I'm guessing that's probably supposed to be shut?" Joey said, and Abi nodded.

Hurrying through, Abi secured the gate behind them. There were no dogs in the grassy area, and the double doors into the hotel were closed, so Abi opened them, hoping nothing had happened while she'd been gone.

But the Doggy Daycare was in absolute chaos. Mel and Rebecca were trying to get the dogs to calm down, but most of them wouldn't stop barking. Aunt Tiffany was checking off each dog by name on her clipboard, and Molly … Molly sat in the corner looking very, very sorry for herself.

"What happened?" Abi asked, and Molly sobbed, running over to her.

"Oh, Abi! I accidentally knocked the gate open and Polka ran out! We can't find her anywhere!"

Joey groaned. "Oh no. We can't tell Maria, not until Polka is back safe and sound. She'll worry and she's not supposed to worry about anything on her wedding day."

Smudge dashed over to butt his head against his owner's hand, and Joey knelt down to pet him. "Hey, boy. At least you stayed put like you were supposed to."

"We'll find her," Aunt Tiffany promised, as she headed over with her clipboard. "I've already got some of the staff looking for her. Luckily, Polka was the only dog to get out — the others are all safely inside. We're going to need to start getting them into their wedding outfits soon, though." She shook her head. "I'm so sorry about all this, Joey."

"Don't worry," Joey said, looking over at Molly and smiling fondly. "These things happen. I know Molly didn't do it on purpose."

"I'm so sorry," Molly said miserably. "But I want to make up for it! I can find Polka, I know I can!"

Abi put her arm around the younger girl's shoulders to try and make her feel better.

"I'll help," Abi said. "Between us, I'm sure we can find one missing dog. Especially one as big and spotty as Polka!"

Molly looked up at her hopefully, and even Lulu barked in agreement.

"OK, then," Aunt Tiffany said. "But hurry — we've only got an hour until the wedding!"

But before Abi and Molly could even make it out of the door, a bridesmaid came rushing in. "Joey, I've been looking for you everywhere. It's a disaster!"

Joey looked alarmed. "What's happened?"

"Maria's lost her grandmother's veil! She's already in her wedding gown, so she can't go looking for it," the bridesmaid said. "She's told me where she's been this morning so I can look for it but I haven't found it yet! Can you help me?"

"Of course," Joey replied.

Abi hopped impatiently from foot to foot. A veil was important, she supposed – but not as important as a missing dog!

"OK," Aunt Tiffany said. "One thing at a time. Joey, you go and help look for the veil." Joey nodded, and led the bridesmaid towards the door, studying the list as he went. "Abi and Molly, you go and search for Polka – and take Lulu with you.

Oh, and a spare lead for Polka too. Mel and I will start getting the dogs dressed, while Rebecca runs the Daycare and looks after the owners coming to collect their pets." She clapped her hands together. "Time to get to work!"

"Where are we going to start?" Molly asked, as she and Abi headed outside again.

Abi thought. "Well, did you see what direction Polka ran off in?"

Molly frowned, her forehead crumpling up as if she was thinking very hard. "She looked like she was sniffing for something. I think she ran towards the woods."

That made sense. Lulu had found lots of fascinating things to sniff at and chase when they'd walked past the edge of the woods earlier.

"Then let's start in the woods," Abi said decisively.

They headed into the trees just behind the

Doggy Daycare, leaves and sticks crunching under their feet as they walked. Abi was trying to go quickly – she knew they didn't have long before Molly would have to go and change into her bridesmaid dress.

"Polka!" Abi called. "Come here, Polka!" She paused for a moment, but there was no answering crash of a dog running through the trees. Abi sighed. Of course it wasn't going to be that easy to find a Dalmatian on the run.

"Maybe Lulu can sniff her out," Molly suggested.

Abi looked doubtfully at her little dog. Lulu was brilliant at many things, and Abi had taught her to follow commands and do simple tricks, but she'd never tried tracking before.

"She's not trained as a tracker," Abi explained. "And she'd need a scent to follow…"

Molly looked so disappointed that Abi

thought it had to be worth a go. "I suppose we can try it."

Crouching down besides Lulu, Abi spoke to the fluffy bichon frise in an excited tone. "Can you smell Polka, Lulu? Find Polka?"

Lulu stared at Abi, her head tilted to the side, as if she were trying to understand.

"Polka?" Abi tried, one last time.

Lulu barked, and dashed off.

Abi grabbed hold of the lead tightly and ran after her, Molly following behind.

But no matter how far into the woods they went, there was still no sign of Polka. Abi suspected Lulu was chasing butterflies and flowers more than Polka's scent. As the little white dog panted to a halt beside a fallen tree, Abi stopped too and sat on the trunk. Molly dropped down to rest beside her.

"It's no good!" Molly said. She rested her elbows on her knees and put her chin in her hands. "I've messed up the whole wedding, when I was only trying to help! Polka and Smudge are supposed to be carrying the rings down the aisle. Now what are they going to do? And Maria is going to be so cross when she finds out that it was all my fault Polka got out in the first place."

"I'm sure she won't," Abi said, hoping it was true. Maria seemed nice – friendly and kind.

"She'll probably decide it's all my fault her veil's gone missing too," Molly went on, grumpily.

"Well, that *can't* be true," Abi said, "because she was wearing it earlier when we had to hide from Joey…" Abi's eyes widened as a thought occurred to her.

She jumped to her feet and Lulu did the same.

Molly just blinked up at her. "What are you doing?"

Abi grinned. "I might not know how to find Polka, but I think I know where Maria's veil is. Come on!"

Chapter Nine

"Where are we going?" Molly asked, as she chased Abi through the woods, back towards the hotel. "What about Polka?"

"We'll keep looking for Polka," Abi promised, "but first, we need to find your sister's veil. Hopefully by then Polka might even have come back for something to eat."

"But how do *you* know where the veil is, when no one else can find it?" Molly skipped forward another couple of steps to catch up.

"Because I saw her wearing it earlier," Abi explained. "Which means she must have lost it after I left her. All we need to do is retrace the steps she took to get back to her room!"

But as it turned out, they didn't even need to do that.

"Do you hear barking?" Molly asked, as they rounded the corner of the hotel by the gardens.

Abi did. She picked up speed as she ran directly toward the bushes where she and Maria had hidden earlier.

"Polka!" she cried with delight, as she saw the bouncy dog barking and jumping round in circle – like she was looking for something, or someone, that wasn't there.

"We found her!" Molly clapped her hands together. "We really, really found her! I helped fix it, just like I said I would!"

"Yes, you did," Abi agreed. "Now, why don't you clip this on to her collar." She handed Molly the spare lead, and the younger girl fastened it on to Polka's collar.

"Phew. Now she can't run off," Molly said.

"As long as you keep a tight hold on that

lead," Abi agreed.

"Shall we take her back to the Daycare now?" Molly asked.

"Not just yet." Abi looked around her, searching for something white in the bushes. Now that they'd found Polka here, Abi was more sure than ever that the veil had to be close by. Maria had explained that Polka might try to escape and find her, and Molly had mentioned that Polka was good at sniffing things out. Could Polka have tried to track Maria's scent?

Polka barked again, straining on her lead as she tried to reach the largest of the pretty flowering bushes. Abi shaded her eyes with her hand as she looked up. There! Right towards the top of the bush was a piece of white lace, streaming out from the greenery and shining in the sunlight. Maria's veil!

"Up there! Can you see it?" Abi pointed towards the veil and Molly looked too.

"Yes, I can!" Molly bounced up and down with excitement. "We really are going to save the day today, aren't we!"

"Only if we can get it down." Abi bit her lip. The veil seemed very high up. "Maria said her veil kept coming loose. It must have slipped off and got caught on one of the branches when she was hiding here from Joey earlier."

"Good job this isn't a rose bush, then," Molly said. "If her veil got ripped by thorns when we tried to get it down, I'd definitely be in trouble again."

Abi strained to try and reach it, but she couldn't.

"I don't think I can get to it on my own. We're going to have to go and get help."

Molly pulled a face. "This is *our* grand rescue. *We* have to get it down."

"But how?" Abi asked.

Molly frowned and wrinkled her freckled nose. Then she gave a little bounce and grinned. "I've got it! I just need to climb on to your shoulders, then I'll be able to reach it and untangle it safely."

"OK," Abi said. "We can try it. But let's tie the dogs' leads to something first. We don't want to lose one of them again!"

Once Lulu and Polka were safely tied up – and looking at Abi and Molly with puzzled expressions – Abi got as close to the bush as she could and crouched down. "Climb up and sit on my shoulders," she told Molly, glad that the younger girl was very small and slight.

Molly did as she was told, swinging one leg either side of Abi's head. "OK, ready," she said.

Slowly and very carefully, Abi stood up, placing her feet a little way apart to help her balance. "That's as high as I can get you. Can you reach it?"

"Almost…" Molly leaned forward a little more, and Abi clung on to her legs to make sure she didn't fall. Abi hoped the veil would still be wearable when they got it back.

"Yes!" Molly said triumphantly. "The comb had just got stuck on a leaf stem. I've freed it now!"

"Great! Then let's get you down." Gently, she lowered Molly to the ground again.

Molly waved the veil around her head, and Abi took it from her before it could meet with any more disasters. After plucking a couple of stray leaves from the lace, she brushed off the dust.

"It was lucky that only the comb got caught," Abi said, studying the veil. "Otherwise the lace might have ripped."

"Hooray!" Molly grinned, and threw her arms around Abi. "We did it! We really did it!"

Abi grinned back. "Yes! Now, let's get Polka – and the veil – back where they both belong." She checked her watch. "And you need to get into your bridesmaid dress!"

Chapter Ten

"You found her! Oh, Abi, well done." Aunt Tiffany took Polka's lead from Abi's hand, and Abi knelt down to let Lulu off her lead too.

"Not just that," Abi said, smiling up at her aunt. "We found Maria's veil as well! Molly's gone to take it back to her."

"You have been busy! I suppose you're ready for a break now, then?" Aunt Tiffany said. "Unless you'd like to help Mel get our doggy guests into their wedding outfits?"

"Of course!" Abi had been looking forward to spending time with all the dogs, and she was eager to get back to helping out.

Mel's dressing-room area was busy, with she and Kim already dressing the dogs. Abi headed over and took the next outfit off the rack, matched it to the correct dog – a spaniel called Bay – and set about easing the dog's paws through the legholes and fastening it tightly under Bay's belly.

Maria and Joey's wedding guests had chosen all sorts of different outfits for their dogs. Some, like Bay, were in doggy versions of a tuxedo, others in tailcoats and little top hats. The girl dogs had colourful dresses, or tutu skirts covered in sequins. And some just had fancy collars or bows, but still looked fabulous. All the dogs seemed excited to be fussed over and primped, ready for the wedding.

Fifteen minutes later, all the other dogs had been claimed by their owners, and only Smudge and Polka were left. There was a knock on the door and in came Molly, wearing her rose-pink bridesmaid dress. After Molly came Maria, her beautiful white wedding dress trailing along the ground behind her. Her veil was neatly pinned on top of her dark curls.

"Abi, I just had to come and say a huge thank you. Molly told me how you found my veil – and my precious Polka."

At the sound of her name, Polka bounded over from where Mel was trying to tie the ribbon with Joey's wedding ring around her neck. As the Dalmatian pawed at Maria's dress, Abi was very glad that Aunt Tiffany had given

Polka such a thorough clean when she came back from her adventure in the gardens!

"I should have realized sooner that your veil had to be in the gardens," Abi said. "If I had, we wouldn't have spent so long searching the woods for Polka!"

"She must have followed my scent," Maria said. "She's such a clever girl," she added, petting Polka again. "And so are you, for thinking to look there. I'd forgotten that I'd hidden there, in all the wedding excitement!"

"Well, I'm glad that everything is back on schedule," Aunt Tiffany said. "But Maria, don't you have a wedding to get to? I was just about to tie your ring on to Smudge and get changed myself, and then I'll be bringing the dogs over for the ceremony."

The Pooch Parlour staff had been invited to watch the wedding ceremony, and they'd all brought outfits to wear for it. Including Lulu and Hugo!

"Then I'd better go," Maria agreed. "But Abi, I was wondering… I know your aunt and her staff will be busy back here later, looking after the dogs while their owners eat dinner, but we have a spare place at Molly's table for the meal, and I'm sure she would like the company…"

Abi looked to Aunt Tiffany for permission, and squealed when she nodded. "I'd love to!"

"Fantastic!" Molly bounced up and down, making her pink skirt swirl out at the bottom. "We're going to have so much fun!"

"Hooray!" Abi looked down at her tunic and leggings. "We'd better all get changed for the ceremony too!"

Everyone was ready just in time to walk over to the wedding with the two Dalmatians. Polka and Smudge looked very smart with their gleaming spotty coats and the pink and blue ribbons around their necks. The wedding rings shone as they hung from the ribbons. But secretly Abi thought that Lulu looked nicest of all, in her sparkly silver tutu dress.

Molly and Aunt Tiffany waited with Smudge and Polka at the entrance for Maria and the other bridesmaids, while Abi hurried through to take a seat in the back row, along with Mel, Rebecca and Kim.

Every chair was filled, and Abi recognized a lot of famous faces. Her eyes grew wide as she spotted a celebrity chef, a film star and a top model – and that was only in one row.

The guests' dogs sat on the pink cushions, proudly showing off their outfits – and investigating their treat bags.

Abi grinned. Maria and Joey must really love all dogs, not just Polka and Smudge, to make them such a big part of their wedding day.

At the front of the chairs, where Joey and his best man were waiting, the string quartet changed their music to something Abi thought she recognized. All the guests stood up, turning to face the back as Molly, in her beautiful rose-pink dress, started walking slowly down the aisle. She scattered pink rose petals as she went, and smiled at Abi as she passed her.

Next came the older bridesmaids, then Polka and Smudge, the golden wedding rings hanging around their necks.

And finally it was Maria's turn. Everyone gasped at her beautiful dress, and Abi thought it looked even more stunning out in the fresh air and sunshine than it had inside the hotel.

At the end of the ceremony, when Maria and Joey kissed as husband and wife, everyone cheered – and the dogs barked their approval.

As the string quartet started playing an orchestral version of one of Maria's songs, the bride and groom walked back down the aisle, Polka and Smudge just ahead of them. Abi smiled. It had been such a beautiful day, and everything had gone perfectly in the end.

As Polka reached their row of chairs, she suddenly darted away from Maria and ran towards Abi! Abi gasped, and tried to turn the big Dalmatian round and send her back to her owner. This wasn't in the wedding plan!

Maria laughed. "You've got a friend for life

in Polka, Abi!" She took Joey's arm again, as Molly appeared at their side holding Polka's lead, ready to clip on to her ribbon. "And in Molly, Joey and me too."

Abi beamed. How often was it that a nine-year-old girl got to make friends with a pop star, a celebrity chef, a disaster-prone bridesmaid and two gorgeous Dalmatians, all in one day?

"That's the best thing about helping out at Pooch Parlour this summer," Abi said. "All the wonderful new friends we've made. Isn't that right, Lulu?"

Lulu barked her agreement and Abi hugged her. Lulu would always be her very best friend.

Did you know....?
Fun facts about Dalmatians!

Dalmatian puppies are born with plain white coats – their first spots normally appear when they are three weeks old.

Dodie Smith, the author of *The Hundred and One Dalmatians*, owned nine Dalmatians – including one called Pongo!

Every Dalmatian's spot pattern is unique. No two pups are the same – like snowflakes!

Pablo Picasso used his pet Dalmatian, Perro, as a subject for his paintings. They're now worth millions of pounds!

Dalmatians' spots aren't always black – they can also be brown, grey, yellow or even blue!

Read the first book in the series

V.I.P.
(Very Important Pup!)

Welcome to Pooch Parlour, where every dog gets star treatment!

Abi is over the moon to be spending the summer at Pooch Parlour, her aunt Tiffany's luxury dog-grooming salon. She can't believe her luck when a famous actress and her adorable Pomeranian Jade appear! Can Abi impress them with the Pooch Parlour pampering treatments?

Jade wants to sparkle!

Read an extract from

V.I.P.

(Very Important Pup!)

Chapter One

"Lulu, we're here!" Abi bounced on her toes as she looked up at the powder-blue door with the words "Pooch Parlour" curling above it in silver letters. "We're really here!"

At her side, Lulu the bichon frise beat her fluffy white tail excitedly against the pavement.

"Should we just go in, do you think?" Abi asked. There was a sign on the door saying "All Dogs Welcome", but there was also one saying "Closed".

Before Abi could decide, Lulu pushed her head against the door, making the bell attached to it chime.

"I guess we're going in!" Abi laughed.

Inside, Pooch Parlour was everything Abi had dreamed it would be. This was her first visit since Aunt Tiffany had moved the parlour to a bigger space in central London.

She'd seen photos online, but they didn't show the pictures of celebrities and their dogs on the walls, or the glass cases displaying every colour of grooming brush, all with sparkly diamonds in the handles.

"Abi, darling. You found us!" Aunt Tiffany appeared through a shimmering curtain behind the reception desk. "So sorry I had to rush off this morning. There's a lot to do before we open for the day! But now I'm all yours, until our first client arrives."

Abi smiled at her aunt as she bent down to unclip Lulu's lead. "That's OK. It *is* only just round the corner." In fact, she could almost see Pooch Parlour from the window of her candy-striped guest bedroom, but Aunt Tiffany had still drawn her a map showing exactly how to get from her flat to the parlour.

When Abi's parents had first told her that she'd be spending the whole summer with Aunt Tiffany, while they were away in America, she'd been nervous. She'd never spent so long apart from her mum and dad before. But Lulu had bumped her head against Abi's hand as if to say, *You'll still have me. We'll be OK*, and Abi realized that as long as she had Lulu with her, she'd never be lonely.

And *then* she'd remembered Pooch Parlour and forgotten to be nervous altogether. A whole summer at Aunt Tiffany's glamorous luxury dog-grooming salon sounded like far too much fun to waste time worrying!

Abi and her mum had filled her best backpack with clothes, and they'd packed all of Lulu's favourite toys in her own bag. And then, yesterday, the day had finally come! Mum and Dad had dropped her off at Aunt Tiffany's, and Abi had hugged and kissed them, too excited to be upset about saying goodbye.

At the flat, Abi and Lulu were welcomed by Aunt Tiffany and Hugo, her miniature dachshund, who'd been wearing his very best tartan dressing gown!

As if he knew Abi was thinking of him, Hugo padded under the shiny pink curtain, dressed today in a stripy blue and white jumper that matched the one Aunt Tiffany was wearing. Lulu gave an excited woof when she spotted him and dashed over to press her nose up against his side. Hugo gave a doggy sigh and stared at Abi with big eyes.

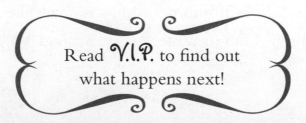

Read **V.I.P.** to find out
what happens next!

Read more from
Pooch Parlour
Dog Star

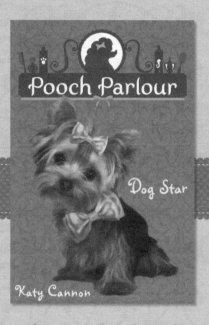

Welcome to Pooch Parlour, where every dog gets star treatment!

When Abi hears that Pooch Parlour
will be the official salon for a group of gorgeous dog stars,
she is thrilled! She will be grooming the most glamorous
pups in town! But can Abi help a perky little
Yorkie called Pickle to get her big break?

Pickle wants to shine!

Read more from
Pooch Parlour
Passion for Fashion

Welcome to Pooch Parlour,
where every dog gets star treatment!

Abi can't wait to join the backstage team at a glittering fashion show for dogs and their owners. But when one of the young models falls ill, Abi is catapulted into the world of catwalks and quick costume changes. Can she handle Boomer, the highly strung pup who will be strutting his stuff by her side?

Boomer wants to dazzle!

How to be a
Pooch-Pampering
Professional!

Dog grooming can be heaps of fun for
both you and your pup – but it's important
to know the right techniques!

Follow our top tips for the perfect pamper:

Make a Splash!

Some pooches love baths, but for others
they can be a bit scary. Try giving your
pup treats in the tub, so he or she
connects water with having fun.

Brush Up!

A dog's coat needs brushing to keep it glossy.
Even if your pup is short-haired like Hugo,
regular brushing will help to remove loose
dead hairs and keep your pooch's fur slick
and clean so they look and feel their best.

Perfect Match!

Find out what kind of brush is right
for your breed of dog. A fluff-ball like
Jade needs a pin brush, whereas a curved
wire brush is best for Lulu's wavy fur.
Ask your breeder or local dog-grooming
parlour for advice.

Smooth Moves!

Sometimes a dog's fur can get tangled
into clumps called "mats", though regular
brushing will help prevent this. If your poor
pup's coat is matted, ask an adult to help you
rub some baby oil into the knots before very
gently combing them out with your fingers.

Natural Beauty!

Dogs come in a range of beautiful colours and it's
best to keep it that way! Dyeing a dog's fur can
cause an allergic reaction, making your pup very
uncomfortable. The staff at Pooch Parlour never dye
a dog's fur – the pups are gorgeous just as they are!

Katy Cannon was born in the United Arab Emirates, grew up in North Wales and now lives in Hertfordshire with her husband and daughter Holly.

Katy loves animals, and grew up with a cat, lots of fish and a variety of gerbils. One of her favourite pastimes is going on holiday to the seaside, where she can paddle in the sea and eat fish and chips!

For more about the author, visit her website:

www.katycannon.com

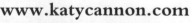